Snowed In For Christmas

Copyright

Second Edition, February 2024
Copyright © 2024 by Melony Ann

Paperback ISBN: 978-1-961966-73-4

Published by: Carxander Publishing
Wisconsin

Opening Quote

I miss you most at Christmas time. And I can't get you, get you off my mind. Every other season comes along, and I'm all right. But then I miss you most at Christmas time.

Miss You Most (At Christmas Time) by Mariah Carey

Chapter One

❄ Nico ❄

"Who the fuck has a wedding on Christmas day?" I ask, glaring at the road in front of me.

"People who really love Christmas," the woman driving the car we're in says without even missing a beat. I'd smile at her for being so quick, but she's the last woman I want to be in this vehicle with.

Noelle Snow.

She's beautiful. Her strawberry-blond hair looks like it was kissed by the sun. Her gray eyes are as bright and as beautiful as her. She's a small woman. Petite, but she has curves in all the right places. I should know. I know her body very intimately. Her ivory skin tone has just enough color for people to know she's not a vampire.

I'm not convinced she's not, though. She's evil enough to be one. I'm sure people think she's the sweetest person to ever walk the face of this Earth, but I know what's underneath. She's crazy. Vindictive. The type of woman who makes a man want to jump off a fucking building and pray for the most painful death imaginable because it would be better than being in her presence for another second.

I glare at her. "Do you even know where you're going?"

She sighs. Loudly. Just the sound of her breathing makes me want to jump out of the car and get hit by a log truck, but it's her dead silence after that sigh that really makes my blood boil. She only does it when she believes whatever I just said is the stupidest thing possible.

I wouldn't even be in this car with her if I had any choice at all. If things had gone my way, I'd be happily stretched out in the first class section of a Delta flight on my way to Denver, Colorado, for my best friend's wedding. I'd be sipping on a beer listening to anything other than the fucking Christmas music floating through the speakers of this silver Ford Fusion piece of shit.

But nope. My flight was canceled to Denver because of a snowstorm. I couldn't even get a flight into any other airport in Colorado and rent a car to drive the rest of the way. Because apparently, the storm is blanketing the entire state. Yeah. My ass. I doubt that very seriously, but again. My life is being controlled by the Government. This time, though, it's not the United States Marine Corp. It's the damn FAA.

"Really, Noelle. Do you know where you're going?" I ask again. I'm getting extremely nervous with the amount of snow coming down right now.

According to my weather app, it's not snowing in Denver. It's underneath Denver. By fucking miles. Which means it should be underneath where we are right now if she's even going the right direction. I shouldn't have handed over the wheel. I shouldn't have fallen asleep. I should've toughed it out and drove straight through.

Noelle lets out an exasperated sigh. "Nico, I'm on the Interstate. Interstate 70 literally drives right into Denver. I know where I'm going. I'm trying to be nice and give you a break from driving. Maybe you should give me one and let me drive. Stop being an ass."

"I'm not trying to be an ass, sweetheart. It's just fucking really snowy right now. The snow is supposed to be below us. That's all."

"First of all. Don't call me sweetheart. You lost that privilege two years ago when you broke up with me. And second. I just passed a sign. It said Interstate 70. So, I'm going by the sign instead of your stupid weather map."

"App."

"Nico! Please shut up!" She takes one hand off the steering wheel to wipe her eyes before she quickly puts it back. I feel the car slow quite a bit. She's white-knuckling the steering wheel. Her attention is focused on the road. As it should be, but I can see how scared she is.

The snow is getting heavier and heavier as the miles go by. Finally, after a few minutes of nothing but the Christmas music, I give in. "Pull over," I say calmly and soothingly. She doesn't need my mood right now.

"I'll be fine. I just need to focus," she says quietly.

"Noelle. I'm not asking. Pull over. Let me take over. You're fucking nervous. I'm a better driver in the snow."

She sniffles. "We live in Las Vegas. We don't get snow there."

"Did you forget that I was born in Vail and lived there most of my life?" I wouldn't put it past her to have forgotten that.

Noelle isn't my biggest fan, but truthfully, I'm not hers either. We were engaged to be married a couple of years ago. We dated for almost two years before I popped the question. During the engagement, I was sent out on my last deployment before my contract with the Marines ended. I didn't plan to re-enlist. I'd already given them almost twenty years of my life. I wanted to settle down. I wanted to turn my part-time job as a police officer with the Las Vegas Police Department to a full-time one.

But mostly, I wanted Noelle. I didn't want her to worry about me being off running missions in countries thousands of miles away. It was enough for her dealing with me being on patrol on the streets of the city. I wanted to ease her fears. She never tried to get me to quit either. That was something she'd never do. It was something I wanted to do for her, though.

When I got home after my deployment, I didn't tell her I was going to be there. I wanted it to be a surprise. I'd even enlisted my brother's help. His only job was to keep her out of the house until I texted him and told him to bring her home.

I was going to make her favorite food, barbecue chicken on the grill with grilled corn on the cob. I even grabbed her favorite fruits, watermelon and cantaloupe, as well as white chocolate covered strawberries drizzled with milk chocolate that had been given a red color. I bought her flowers, a gorgeous Spring bouquet, and stopped off at the jewelry store to grab her the necklace she wanted but wouldn't buy for herself, no matter how many times I told her to. It was on a silver chain and had a hummingbird charm.

6

When I pulled into the driveway, I expected to see her car parked there. I didn't expect to see Christian's, my brother's. It was at that very moment my stomach sank. My feet carried me into the house. It was dead silent. I put all of the groceries and flowers on the counter before making my way through the house.

That's when I saw it. My beautiful fiancè in our bedroom wrapped in nothing but a fluffy, white towel sitting on our bed.

And my fucking brother with his head between her thighs.

I lost it. Noelle didn't even have the decency to get up and say anything for herself. It was my brother who stood up. My brother who told me it wasn't what it looked like. My brother who said she'd sprained her ankle. My brother who said I was early. That he hadn't gotten a chance to take her out yet.

Those words took on a whole new meaning then.

It took everything in me not to choke him out. Not to pummel him until he was nothing more than a bloody pile of steaming dog shit. Instead, I turned around and walked out. I texted her and told her to leave. She did as she was told, but not before both her and Christian texted me and called me a thousand times. I never answered either of them and blocked them both after she was gone. Christian tried again and again to talk to me, but I refused.

It's been a little more than two years since that day. I almost said fuck it and re-enlisted. I chose not to and stuck with my original plan. I became a full time cop with LVPD, and I love it. I don't need her. I don't need Christian. I'm good.

I feel Noelle start sliding and quickly reach over to help her before she starts spinning. She screams and lets go of the wheel at the same time she takes her foot off the gas and curls into herself like she's bracing herself for a crash.

"Hands on the wheel!" I snap. She immediately puts her hands on the wheel, but she's still screaming. "Stop, Noelle! Hands on the wheel!" I realize the mistake of my words far too late.

Noelle grips the wheel like I told her to, but she also stomps on the brakes. I had us out of the spin, but she put us right back into one. Before I know what's happening, we're spinning in circles. Noelle is screeching and crying. My heart starts racing, but before I can tell her to take her foot off the brake, I see a wall of white coming right at us…

Chapter Two

❄ Noelle ❄

I could've already been safe in my hotel room. Instead, the FAA grounded my flight. I don't even know why I accepted the invite to this wedding. I shouldn't have bothered. I knew Nico would be there. Aaron, the groom, is Nico's best friend. Nico is supposed to be his best man. If I'd listened to myself and chosen the better option of skipping this, I'd be home warm in my bed instead of buried in a giant snowbank with the one person in this world that I truly despise.

I refuse to burst into tears like I want to. I wipe my eyes and look around. The airbags have deployed. I'm thankful for that. My chest hurts, but I'm sure the airbags cushioned us from the hard crash.

Other than the airbags, I see nothing around us but piles of white with a dark backdrop. The snow falling makes everything look gray. The last time I remember looking at the time, it was 1:37 in the morning. The snow is coming down like sheets of rain. It's quickly blanketing us. Thankfully, the car is still running. That means we won't freeze. Right?

The windshield wipers are still going.

The lights are still on, though the front end is smashed to hell. I guess it's lucky the headlights work at all.

Suddenly, the airbag deflates with a soft pop. I jump a little, then see Nico stabbing his own with his pocket knife. His expression is dark and even more angry than it was when he got it in his stupid mind that I was cheating on him. With his brother of all people. I blink the tears away and turn so I'm not looking at him. I have to figure out how to survive this disaster.

I take a breath and search for my cellphone. It's on the floor at my feet. I unbuckle my seatbelt and reach down to pick it up. I quickly open my internet and wait for it to load.

And wait…

And wait…

And wait…

"You think you're getting reception out here?" Nico asks, his voice low and gravelly. I hate him. I hate what his asshole voice does to me.

I refuse to allow my body to shiver, but it doesn't stop my bitch of a pussy from becoming a traitorous jerk.

I ignore him and keep trying as he looks at me both amused and furious. Unfortunately, he's right. I'm not getting any reception at all. I can't even send a text or make a call. I bite my lip when emergency calls won't even go through.

Okay. Stay calm. It's okay. You have heat. You have warm clothing in the back. The snow should stop soon. We can get out and make a call then. I've always been told to stay in the car in bad weather. If I get too wet or cold, I could get hypothermia and die.

I nod resolutely to myself and start climbing into the backseat.

"What are you doing?" Nico asks, exasperated.

I ignore him and keep going. "If I can get to the clothing, we can layer up and stay warm. The back seats have a safety feature in case you get stuck in the trunk. We have to stay warm. We might be here for a little while until the snow stops. We can get help then."

He wraps one of his muscular arms around my waist and stops me in my tracks. "Do you really not keep up with anything? This storm is supposed to be the storm of the century, Noelle! We stay in the fucking car, we're going to get buried alive. Just sit down and let me fucking figure out where the hell we are." He nearly shoves me back into my seat, then reaches into the back for his backpack. He takes out something that looks like a phone, but it's thicker and Army green.

I huff. "No reception. Remember?" I cross my arms over my chest and chew my lip as I glare out the window.

"Satellite. I'm a fucking Marine. Remember?" His tone is just as cocky as it is mocking and condescending. I stay quiet. "We're a couple of miles out of Genesee Park. There's a cabin near here. It's mine. About a mile in from the Interstate. We're about a hundred feet from the access road." He pauses and gives me a jerk of a grin along with his stupid glare. "Nice place to crash, Ace."

"Asshole," I grumble.

He shrugs. "I've been called worse. Let's go." He pulls the handle to open his door, but it doesn't budge.

"I'm not going anywhere."

He pushes the lock button and tries again. "Motherfucker." He tries again, slamming his entire, beautiful body into the door. Nico Jasper, everyone. He thinks he can get anything he wants through brute force.

I sigh. That's not fair. He's never been an abusive person. Nico isn't like that. He can be scary. He's almost six feet four. He's solid muscle. Titanium. Impenetrable. The hair on his head and stubble on his jaw is as dark as his nearly coal colored eyes. He has a few tattoos on his arms, but it's the wings on his back that have always made my mouth water. It's because he had always been my angel. He's an angel to everyone he loves.

That all ended for us long ago. Maybe it's because I'm too young. I'm not trustworthy yet or something. He's thirty-seven. I'm barely twenty-six. I have a good job as a casino host. I worked my way up to that position from a hotel receptionist. I graduated at the top of my class in high school and college.

Nico was in the military when I was still in high school. He got a part-time police officer position with Las Vegas PD. He wanted it that way because he never quite knew when he'd get deployed. I met him when he showed up on a call at the casino. We hit it off. We were together for almost three years before he decided it would be fun to destroy my life. I was only twenty-four then. Since he broke up with me, I've thrown myself into work. I became the best employee I could be and moved up quickly.

He has no idea how badly he tore me and Christian, his brother, up. He doesn't care anyway. He blocked us both from his life just as easily as he did from his phone. He didn't care to know what really happened.

We both know how it looked, but the fact that he refused to listen to either of us is what hurt the most. It still does.

I jerk my head to him when I feel cold air hit me. My eyes widen. "Oh my God! What are you doing?" I screech.

He pauses and looks at me. "I'm getting the fuck out of here before your gas is gone and we end up freezing to death. Come if you want. Or don't. I don't give a fuck."

"Nico! You're going to freeze out there!" I nearly squeak as he pulls himself out of the window he opened.

He pauses when his feet hit the ground and looks back in at me. He shrugs so nonchalantly that it infuriates me. I nearly scream. "Guess that's my problem. Put the window up and pop the trunk so I can get my stuff."

I don't hold back the scream. I push the button so the window goes up and push the button for the trunk. "Fine! If you want to die, it's not my problem!" I scream again just because of how frustrated, angry, and upset I am. Screaming keeps me from crying.

I close my eyes and do all I can to regulate my breathing. I don't need to start panicking. It's not going to help me. I need to be calm and rational. That's what's gotten me through most of my life.

That goes out the window the second my headlights go out. The car starts to sputter. My eyes drop in horror to my gas gauge. It's close to empty.

"No... No! No! No!"

I jump nearly a mile when Nico slams the trunk closed. It's all it takes for the car to die.

My heart shoots into my brain and fights to escape through my head.

My lungs stop inflating.

I gasp for air. I feel the oxygen going into my mouth and down my throat, but it doesn't seem to be doing anything more. I don't even know if my heart is pumping.

I quickly try to open the door, but like Nico's door, mine doesn't budge no matter how many times I throw myself into it. It hurts my chest even more because of the airbag deploy, but I don't care. I have to get out.

The window! He climbed out the window!

I quickly hit the button. Even if the key is turned but it's not running, it should go down.

As soon as I hit it, though, I realize just how wrong I am. I can't see the front of the car anymore, but I can see there's smoke coming from under the hood.

"Oh my God! Nico!" I scream. The wiring. It has to be on fire! Is that why the car shut down?

I start pounding on the window, praying it'll break.

It's then I see the silver glint of something next to me and snow flying, but I can't figure out what's happening. My mind is solely on the fact that I'm stuck in a car that's going to blow up at any given moment.

Unable to stop them, the tears I was fighting burst from my eyes. I start frantically searching for anything that will break the window. Nico has to be long gone right now. He's not going to help me.

He'd probably leave me in the car to die.

He hates me that much…

Chapter Three

❄ Nico ❄

I shake my head and keep shoveling snow away from Noelle's door. There's no point in trying to calm her down. She's thrown herself into a panic. It took me a few moments to realize what the fuck she was screaming about. Then I noticed steam coming off her hood. She probably thinks there's a fire. I don't think she was quite out of gas, though she was nearing empty. It's more likely the battery shorted out.

She's lucky I'm too fucking nice to leave her ass here. I'd never be able to live with myself, though. The snow is heavy. It's already almost up to the window on her side. It's not stopping anytime soon either. This storm was supposed to hit tomorrow afternoon. Not today. It was one of the reasons I was so pissed off they canceled the flight. I saw nothing anywhere that said it was snowing right then in Denver. Even the news they had on in the airport said it hadn't started.

I almost called my buddy and told him I'm not making it, but Noelle is some kind of angel. I didn't know she was at the damn airport, let alone the same flight as me. While I was arguing and trying to force my way onto any other flight flying into Colorado, Noelle was smartly booking a rental. It's only about a twelve hour drive from Las Vegas to Denver.

I started out driving but started to get tired a few hours ago. I haven't been sleeping too well lately. Sometimes, some of the shit I saw overseas hits me hard. The past few days, I guess it's just that time. Maybe it's because one of our friends didn't make it home.

I shovel a little more vigorously as Noelle cries. Maybe the reason I haven't been sleeping is because we lost him on this day two years ago. Aaron and I were home three weeks later, both having made the decision not to reenlist. Who knew my fucking life would just keep unraveling before my very eyes?

Of course, Aaron has been on Noelle's side this whole time. He's never shoved it down my throat, but I know he continues to talk to her. He told me as much. He'd even told me I should talk to her a few times, but I refused.

I should be grateful to Noelle for getting me this far. I won't miss Aaron's wedding. It's been the most awkward fucking drive, though. Neither of us have said more than a few words to each other. The most we've spoken was at the airport when she said she got the last car rental. If my truck wasn't in the shop, I wouldn't have taken her up on the offer. I even made her wait until after I tried booking a private flight.

No dice.

And now here we are. Her rental is going to be buried within the hour. The temps are dropping fast. I pulled her stuff out with mine when I went into the trunk. I've never been more grateful that I bought this shovel from the gas station we stopped at when I turned the wheel over to her. She rolled her eyes, but I never ignore instincts. The storm was underneath us and stalled, but I'm always prepared. It's what Marines do.

After I get the snow shoveled enough for her to get out. I yank open the door. She screams, and I almost fall backwards. I guess I didn't realize she was in full panic mode until right now. Maybe I should have tried to comfort her.

"Noelle, it's okay. I -" I'm cut off by her leaping out of the car. I have to step back to balance us both before I land on my ass in the snow with her on top of me.

"It's going to blow!"

"What?" I shake my head. "It's just steam, Noelle. From the melted snow and the warm hood. You probably didn't notice it until the battery shorted and the car shut down." I hug her closer and tighter as she gasps and sobs, trying to help herself come down. I want to shove her away, but not even I'm that big of an asshole.

"I'm sorry," she chokes out as she lets go after a few moments. She sniffles. "I… didn't mean to do that."

I drop my arms from her body and ignore my reaction to her. I hate that she's the only woman who has ever set my body ablaze like this. One look, and she has my dick trying to escape my jeans, but the second I feel her against me, it's all over. There's no hiding the erection. If he could stand at full attention and salute, he would do it just as if she was the fucking General.

I clear my throat and move her out of the way. "Don't be." I lean in the car and grab our stuff from the back.

We both have coats on the seat as well as what we would have carried onto the plane, boots included. She was smart. She knew she was flying into a city that was likely to have snow. Her tennis shoes wouldn't cut it. I put the bags on top of the luggage.

"How are we going to carry all of that? Where are we even going?"

"I have a cabin around here. I told you that already. I planned to stay there. It's only about twenty minutes from the city. I have a buddy check on it from time to time for me when I'm not there, but I go there when I need a break from Vegas or life. It's a peaceful retreat. I knew I'd be getting in late so I texted him after we left and asked him if he could stock me up with food and stuff, then sent money via Venmo. I didn't know if I'd be able to get fully stocked up before the storm hit. I told him I'd be there really early in the morning. He texted me a couple of hours later and told me I was all set. If we can get there before you freeze, we'll be good."

She shakes her head. "Because I'm incapable of a hike, right? Nothing but an airhead city girl."

I sigh as I turn to her. "I didn't say that, Noelle. You're fucking five feet nothing on a good day. You've lost a lot of weight since…" I trail off and shake my head. "Fuck it. Sure. I meant you're an airhead city girl. Sit down and put your boots on."

Her lip trembles, but she wisely doesn't say a damn word. I already changed into my boots, but I throw my coat on and hold out hers when she's done changing into the boots. I put her shoes into my backpack while she puts her coat on.

"So, how are we getting to your cabin? There's no way we can hike out of here. The snow is up to my waist," she says quietly, defeated almost. It might break my heart if I weren't already fed up with her.

I point to the road. "We cross it. We walk down the access road. Viola." She nods and starts grabbing her bag. I shake my head. "I'll take it."

"I can take my own stuff. I don't want to put you out more. I already almost killed you by my own stupid driving and panic." She gestures to the totaled car.

I sigh and pinch the bridge of my nose. "Stop, Noelle. You hit ice. You're not used to this. I should've made you pull over sooner. Let's go."

I'm grateful she packed a duffel bag instead of a suitcase. It's easier for me to carry. I put my backpack on, then put her bag and mine over my shoulders, one on each side, before helping her with her own carry on. It's a smaller duffel bag, but I'm impressed that she packed so efficiently.

I turn and lead her up to the road. For a busy Interstate, I haven't seen any vehicles. I'm pretty sure that's because a travel ban was put in place. If I could get some kind of internet signal for my phone, I'd know.

We hike in silence for a while. To her credit, Noelle says nothing. I've taken quick glances back at her, and even with the snow piling up quickly, she's trudging through like a trooper. I can't help but notice that she's shivering pretty uncontrollably, though.

We're only about half way, and I'm starting to question if she'll make it before she freezes. The snow is lashing down like sleet at us. Despite the hood on her head, she's soaked. The coat is waterproof. So are the boots. Her jeans, though, aren't, and she's a lot shorter than me.

I glance behind her when I hear what I'm hoping is a plow. It will make things a fuck of a lot easier for her if it is. I quickly grab the flashlight I put in my pocket before we left the car. I turn it on and stop. Noelle nearly runs into me since she's hunkered into her coat with her head down.

I steady her from falling as I shine the flashlight at the vehicle and start moving it back and forth on the road. I want to warn the driver that we're here so he doesn't hit us, but mostly, I want him to stop. Noelle isn't going to make it, and I'm actually starting to feel like shit about it. Fuck my heart and morals.

"W-w-what's h-h-hap-p-pening?" she says between chattering teeth. She tries to glance around her but coughs instead.

"I'm hoping this is a plow, and he can drive us the rest of the way."

"I c-c-can m-m-make it."

I chuckle at her tenacity, but I know she's just trying to be brave and prove me wrong. I let out a relieved breath when the plow slows down.

The person in the passenger seat pops his head out the window with a grin. "What the hell are you doing out here, Marine? Need a new challenge?"

I bark out a laugh. "No, asshole. We spun out on I-70. Our rental is probably buried right now."

Jim, the older man in the passenger seat who also owns a general store in town, nods. "East or West?"

"West. We were just heading into town. Hit some ice. Spun out and got buried in the snow in the ditch. When we got out, the car was half buried already."

"I'll send one of my guys out in the morning when this shit lets up. We're gonna get hit again, hard, but we'll have about an hour window," the driver, Ted, says. He owns a small auto shop in town. He and his team are the only tow truck drivers.

"Appreciate it, man. Thanks," I say with a nod. "Think you can get us to the cabin? She's pretty cold." I tilt my head towards Noelle. As if on cue, she hugs herself even tighter than she already was and shivers violently.

"Absolutely," Jim says. "Hop on in. Not a lot of room, though. She'll have to sit on your lap." He waggles his eyebrows, but my stomach sinks. I just nod as he opens the door.

I start handing him our stuff so he can put it in the small space behind the seats. He slides over. I climb into the cab and reach out a hand for Noelle. She looks at it for a moment before gauging how hard it'll be for her to get into the truck on her own. Finally, she takes my hand and lets me pull her into my lap. If she weren't shivering so violently, she might choose Jim's over mine. Fuck, the option ain't off the table. I'd happily let her.

Instead, I close the door and keep my arms to myself. It's enough that every shiver makes her ass press against my dick. Sometimes, she jerks. When Ted hits a bump, it's even worse. I have to fight myself to keep the groan tamped down. My cock sure as hell isn't cooperating with my commands to tone it the fuck down.

Her being this close to me is torture, but having her in the same house as me as we ride out this storm is going to be pure hell.

Chapter Four

❄ *Noelle* ❄

We've been at Nico's cabin for a couple of hours. The sun is just starting to rise. I'm so tired, but I can't fall asleep because I'm still so cold. He was nice enough to make us hot chocolate. He even started a fire in his fireplace. Whoever his friend is, he was nice enough to not only stock up his fridge and cabinets with food, but he also brought him enough wood for the fireplace to last weeks.

Even though I've been as close to the fireplace as I can possibly be without being inside it, I can't get warm. Nico even gave me the thickest blanket he has, which was the comforter off his own bed. It's no use.

"I'm actually starting to worry about you," Nico mumbles from the longer couch across from me. The one I'm on is a loveseat that he's moved closer to the fire.

I shiver. "C-can't s-stop." I close my eyes and sniffle.

Nico stretches as he shifts onto his side. "Come here."

My eyes widen at him. "I'm f-f-fine."

"You know if you don't do what I tell you, I'm just going to make you."

I shake my head and snuggle more under the comforter. "It's r-really f-fine."

"Noelle. Come on. Seriously. You're cold. Everything I've tried so far isn't helping. Including giving you a pair of my sweats and my sweatshirt that I warmed up in the dryer. I've given you hot chocolate. I've made sure that fire is roaring. Get over here. I can't get you to the hospital, and you're nearing hypothermia stages at this point. Your lips are blue, and I know it ain't lipstick because you hate makeup. Let me use my body heat to help warm you up. It's not like you haven't been in my arms before."

"Th-that w-was before you f-fucked up."

"Before I fucked up?" He barks out a laugh that's filled with such an intense level of anger and hurt that I briefly forget about how cold I am. His reaction takes me aback. "Just get over here, Noelle. Trust me. I don't want to be anywhere near you. I hate you as much as you hate me, but I can't handle watching you die when I know I can help. Just do it, or I'll just walk over there, pick you up, and bring you over here myself."

I just stare at him in open-mouthed shock, but I do what he says because I don't want to shiver anymore. I know how serious hypothermia can be. So, I take a breath and throw the comforter off me. I stomp the few steps to the couch and lay next to him with my back to him as I throw the comforter over us both.

Almost instantly, and much to my dismay, I feel warmer. His body heat against mine feels way too familiar. Too comforting. I close my eyes as he adjusts the comforter. He wraps his arms around me and pulls me as close to his body as he can. He locks his arms around me, forcing me to relax as he wraps around me.

We say nothing for I don't know how long, but he never moves. His steady breathing, as it always has, lulls me into a state of comfort I haven't felt for a long time. For the millionth time over the past two years, I think to myself how there is nothing in this world that can compete with him and the way he makes me feel. The thought, as it normally does, makes me tear up. Nico was supposed to be my ride or die. Why did some stupid misunderstanding have to ruin all of that?

I force the thoughts away and close my eyes. I let my imagination wander. For a few moments, or even hours, I fall asleep thinking of him as mine again.

❄ ❄ ❄

When I wake up, I'm not sure how long I've been asleep, the fire is nothing but embers. It takes me a few seconds to reorient myself, but when I do, I can't help melting into Nico. I'm not meant to be with anyone else. Nico is it for me. I have to convince him of that. I can't live without him. Being with him like this has made me realize it. Everything he's done since we left the airport has been nothing but selfless.

Purely Nico Jasper.

My Marine.

The thoughts being in his arms elicits quickly fade. He's not mine anymore. He hates everything about me. He's too stubborn to listen to reason. He's the one who broke me in a million tiny pieces. So many that I still haven't managed to put myself together again. I'm like Humpty Dumpty. Nothing can fix me, and if I really think I'm going to do whatever it takes to prove to him that I'm not who he thinks I am, well, I'm sure the rejection will shatter me more.

The question really becomes if I'm willing to risk it all again. I'm already fragile. I still haven't healed. My love for Nico was hotter than the hottest fire. I thought that's how he felt for me, too. I guess I was wrong.

Feeling more like myself, warm on the outside, dead on the inside, I shift against him just enough so I can sit up. What I don't expect is his face to bury itself deeper in my hair. I certainly don't expect his solid as the hardest diamond cock to push closer to my ass. But it's when his arms and legs tighten around me that I gasp.

"Nico," I whisper.

He groans. "Just give me a minute. You owe me that."

My eyes widen on their own. My heart beats faster. I can't lay here like this with him. It's too dangerous. My body isn't on the same page as my head. I try to get up, but my body obeys his raspy-voiced command and sinks into him even more. It takes the full minute he asked for before my body catches up with the conclusion my brain has already reached.

I push myself up, ignoring the sudden chill of not being in his arms. "I *owe* you that?"

Nico growls and turns his head into his arm before glaring up at me. "I don't know. For saving your life? Keeping you warm? Keeping you from being buried in snow? Oh! How about this one? For fucking my brother while I was deployed." His coal eyes manage to darken impossibly more, but his voice is as smooth as the finest butter.

Which does nothing more than get on my last nerve. I should scream. I should haul off and slap him with every ounce of strength I have. I don't. Instead, I stand up and say nothing. I try to hide the hurt his words inflict, but I can't. My face falls. My body droops. I stalk off to his bedroom at the back of the cabin.

"What's the matter, baby girl? Can't handle the truth?" Nico calls after me.

I can hear the humor in his voice, and that's what cuts me the deepest. The scars from the pieces I managed to stitch back together are torn open once more. My heart lays at my feet. Each beat seems to get slower and slower until it finally stops.

I rummage through my clothing, still in my bag, until I find the warmest stuff I packed. Maybe if I put leggings on underneath my jeans, I'll stay warmer longer as I'm trekking through the snow. Nico said he was a couple of miles or something out of town. Maybe if I can make it to the town, I'll be able to find someplace to stay and ride out the rest of the storm. Then, I can call Christian to come get me. He was smart and flew into Denver two days ago. I wish I'd been able to book a flight sooner. I was honestly lucky I got the one I did. Who knew it would get canceled?

I let out a breath as I take the clothes out of the bag. I plan to leave the clothes I was wearing yesterday here because they're still in the dryer. I just want to leave. It was foolish of me to think for a moment there was any chance of reconciliation between us. I'd rather live with the knowledge of knowing he was the one that got away over trying to work it out with someone who hates me as much as he does.

I glance out the window. The snow is coming down heavier than it was last night. That sucks a lot for me, but hopefully if I follow the main roads, I'll get there.

I take Nico's sweatshirt off and put a bra on. I can already feel the biting air. The fireplace is wonderful, but it doesn't heat the entire cabin. I do my best to block the cold air from my mind. I start to think of warm beaches and sand. Anything to keep the precious body heat I have.

The heat he gave me.

I'm reaching for a long-sleeve under shirt and my sweater just as the door starts to open. Like it's on a swivel, my head snaps to the door. My eyes land on Nico's dark gaze. He leans against the doorframe and crosses his arms over his unfairly broad chest.

"What are you doing?" His eyes drop from mine and land on the bag on the bed I haven't zipped up.

My gaze, though, is completely frozen on him. My mouth goes dry, and I stop mid-motion. No words formulate. I feel like I just got caught by my dad trying to sneak out of the house. I'd expect my heart to be racing right now.

Only this time, it doesn't. It feels nothing. Maybe his words earlier really did kill me this time...

Chapter Five

❄ Nico ❄

For several moments, I stand in the doorway watching Noelle. She looks like a deer in the headlights. Like she was just caught doing something wrong. Her expression is a mix between bewildered and pissed.

My breath catches. She's still the most beautiful woman I've ever seen. She's standing in her pajama bottoms and a red bra that I know she bought for my eyes only. I was there when she tried it on. She was as red as the bra with embarrassment at the fact that her ample breasts spilled out of it.

It took a store associate to explain to her that it was supposed to be like that. It's meant to push her tits up and give her a sexy amount of cleavage. The support is the perfect amount, and what she considers spilling out is really just the bra making her more sexy than she's used to.

I narrow my eyes for two reasons. The first is because I want to know why the fuck she packed that bra, and why she's wearing it right now. The second is because I'm pissed she even still has it. It was supposed to be just for the two of us. She only ever wore it when she wanted to sexily seduce me. The very thought she's wearing it for any other reason infuriates me.

"Of all the bras you own, Noelle, why that one?" I pinch the bridge of my nose and close my eyes, breaking the spell between us. I can hear her clothes rustling as she changes.

"I can wear what I want. You're not going to have to worry anyway."

I bark out a bitter laugh as I open my eyes again. Unfortunately for me, she's got her sweater on. My dick is as unhappy about that as I am. "Where do you think you're going? Out there?" I gesture towards the window. "You'll drown in the snow. It's almost up to my windows. Which, just so you know, are four feet above the ground. And let's not talk about the fact that you'll fucking freeze to death and won't be found until the snow melts."

She shrugs. "Then, I guess that's my problem." She starts shoving the clothes she removed from her body into the bag after throwing my own words from last night back at me. She zips her bag..

My jaw ticks. I don't take well to my words being thrown back at me. She knows that. "You're not leaving, Noelle."

She turns her own furious glare on me. Her gray eyes are as stormy as it is outside. "You can't keep me here. I can do whatever I want. You lost the privilege of being my dom and telling me what to do when you accused me of cheating on you."

I scoff. "Kind of hard to accuse you of anything when I saw it with my own eyes! It's not an accusation at that point. It's a fucking fact!"

She picks up her bag and slings it over her shoulder. Her face is red with anger. Her eyes look like they could pierce the strongest armor. "I never cheated!" she screams at me. "Just because I'm twelve years younger than you doesn't mean I don't have morals and can't control my impulses! Which I never had for your brother or anyone else!"

She storms towards me and forces her small body past me. The only reason she succeeds is because I'm taken aback by not only her outburst, but her blatant as fuck denial. I follow her as she stomps towards the front door. She's quick for someone as tiny as she is, but I catch up to her before she gets too far.

I grab her arm and spin her around before dropping my hand from it like she just scalded me. I can feel my own fury building. "How the fuck can you deny any of this? I saw it! I saw you sitting on that bed wrapped in a towel with Christian's head between your legs!"

25

"I never cheated!" she screams. "I hurt my ankle getting out of the shower! I slipped! I practically knocked myself unconscious! Did you know he took me to the hospital after that? No! Because you were too busy being an asshole to us! You were too high on your horse and too fucked up to even talk to us! No matter how many times we tried! You completely destroyed us, Nico!"

"The fuck I did! You hurt your ankle my ass! It didn't look like he was looking at your fucking ankle!"

Tears pool in her eyes, but I'm not sure if they're from the fact that my words finally cut through her and she knows she can't deny facts, or if it's because she's furious I'm not falling for any of the bullshit.

She doesn't say a word. She drops her bag and reaches into the back pocket of her jeans. She unlocks her phone and thrusts it into my chest with a force that might hurt anyone else.

"Fuck you, Nico. You can keep the phone. If I'm gonna die out there, I may as well do it right. ,A stupid woman rushes out into the storm of the century without a phone to call for help'." She laughs wryly and emotionlessly. "I can see the headlines now."

I take the phone with no intention of actually looking at it. She's not leaving the house. She won't need the damn phone anyway, but as I'm about to throw it against the wall, something catches my eye. I pause as she picks up her bag and continues to the door. I look at the image she pulled up of someone's foot. Hers. I'd know it anywhere. I don't even have to see my name tattooed on the lower part of her leg.

It's obvious she sprained it. So obvious. It's bruised to hell and swollen to the size of a damn baseball. "Come on, Noelle. How the fuck do I know this wasn't last month?"

"You know, I knew you'd ask that. It's the stubborn cop in you. So, go ahead. Swipe up. Look at the details. It shows you when the image was taken. And after that, swipe left. You'll see several more images. One of them is when I was in the hospital."

"Again -"

She cuts me off like I hadn't even tried to say a word. "If you look closely on the one with the silly selfie with me and Christian, you'll see the computer in the background. It shows the date right on there."

"Noelle -"

Again, she rolls right over me like I hadn't attempted to speak. She continues to put her boots on, not looking at me at all. "Oh. And before you say anything about how happy we both look together, keep in mind that I'd just lost you. I had a concussion. It wasn't just a sprain, it was broken. And I'd fractured my wrist during the fall. I was anything but happy. You'll see that if you look closely enough. I appreciate your brother, though. He really tried to help me through all of that."

I do what she says and scroll through, but only out of purely morbid curiosity. As she said, the images are all date stamped with the very day I walked away. The emergency room images are the same. One of the images, I can see her wristband. It has the date and time she checked in. The image of her with my brother, though, is the one that breaks my heart. While they both are trying to act silly, I can see just how upset and hurt they are. Their eyes look dead.

Kind of like how Noelle's look right now.

I'm starting to panic.

Fuck…

What did I do?

Fuck… Fuck! Fuck!

I need to fix this.

I'll talk to Christian later. Right now, I need to make this right with Noelle.

My girl.

I take a deep breath to stop the rising dread. "Noelle, stop." I drop her phone on the couch and walk towards her.

She shakes her head and holds up a hand. "Don't. Don't do this. I'm barely holding on, Nico. I've been clinging to a thread for a long time. It's frayed and about ready to break. I can't fight with you anymore. Every time I look at you, I feel like I might actually die from the hurt." She swallows a sob and closes her eyes, but doesn't drop her hand.

I reach out slowly and take it. It's trembling; all of her is. I did this. I broke us both because I walked in on something I couldn't process. I didn't listen when our friends tried to talk to me. I didn't listen to my parents. More importantly, I didn't listen to Christian and Noelle. I didn't listen to reason. I believed I knew what I saw and didn't give a shit about what either of them were telling me. I thought it was just two people trying get out of fucking up after being caught redhanded in said fuck up.

I should've listened.

I pull her closer, keeping her hand in mine, and cup her cheek with the other. "Noelle, I'm so sorry, baby girl."

She shakes her head, the tears finally spilling as she pulls her hand free. She takes several steps back. "You don't get to call me that anymore! And you don't get to apologize after this long and expect everything will be fine!" She grabs her coat and starts putting it on.

My chest actually fucking tightens at the very thought of her walking away from me. What's more, though, is the panic I feel at her being out in the storm. I can't handle the idea of anything happening to her. I thought it was because I'm just that kind of person, and it might have something to do with it, but it has a lot more to do with the fact that I care about her. No matter what I tell myself, I've never stopped loving her.

I can't.

She's the other part of my soul. The piece I never knew was missing until she was gone. The anger and hurt filled the void for a little while, but the second I heard her sweet, soft, and very hesitant voice behind me in the airport, that was it. I felt the black void more prevalently than I've ever felt anything in my life. I took her up on her offer to drive out here and share the car she rented not because I had no other choice. It was because I didn't want another one. I wanted to spend time with her again. My heart needed it.

Trust that fucker to know exactly what I need when my mind is being a stubborn fucking dickhead.

I take a deep breath as she slings her bag over her shoulder again and turns for the door. She yanks it open, but I slam it shut again. "Noelle. No. I'm not letting you go out there in this. I'm fucking not letting you go, period."

She turns towards me. Mistake number one on her part. I cage her against the door and lock it as my gaze meets her piercing stare. Mistake number two for her. She's fucking sexy when she's pissed, and since I woke up with her in my arms, I haven't been able to get my cock, or the rest of me, to behave.

"You can't keep me here against my will. It's called kidnapping."

"Wrong. It's called saving your fucking life. If you go out there, you will freeze. You won't make it to town. The snow is too deep. You come across a drift, it will be taller than you. I'm certain they pulled the plows, but in the rare case some asshole is out there driving in this shit, and you, by some rare miracle manage to make it to the Interstate, you will be hit. You *will not* be seen in time for someone to stop. And that's only if the plows haven't been pulled. Judging from how much snow has fallen, though? They have. Realistically, you're not making it ten feet out that door."

She pushes as hard as she can against me, but this time, I don't budge. And that is her final mistake. Three strikes. I'm done fucking around. I grab both of her wrists and use my body to pin her against the door. I lean down and kiss her with a level of passion I've been holding back since the day I walked away.

The second my lips meet hers, I'm a goner. I make a solemn vow to fix everything I fucked up because I can't live my life without her.

As I swipe my tongue over hers after forcing my way into her sexy mouth, she watches me with wide eyes. I know one thing. If she's done with me for good, I won't survive it.

Chapter Six

❋ Noelle ❋

The first thing I feel when Nico starts kissing me like I'm his air and he'll die without me, is a sense of calm wash over me. Like it's all going to be okay again. Like everything I've ever wanted to happen is happening. Our reunion. Us getting back together. All of the love I once had for him that has never died. It's multiplied exponentially until the weight of it nearly crushes me.

The second thing I feel is the overwhelming anger I've had for him for a long time. The sense of betrayal I've felt at the very idea he could possibly think I'd ever do something to hurt him. The pain that he bestowed single-handedly on my heart the very moment he showed he didn't trust me.

While I want to throw my arms around him and kiss him just as deeply and passionately as he is me, the simmering anger wins out. I pull away quickly with narrowed eyes. My hand moves on its own and connects with his face. Hard.

His head snaps to the side. It's like he moves in slow motion as he turns back to me. At first, his eyes register shock before fury. The low growl that comes from the pit of his stomach sounds demonic. While I should be terrified, I'm not. I'd be lying if I said I'm not slightly turned on.

"I'll let that slide because I deserve it," he says low and dangerously. "Do it again, though, I'm taking you over my knee."

My eyes widen, and my pussy clenches. Just the memory of being over his knee and the deliciousness that came from it has my panties melting off my body. My mouth both waters and becomes as dry as the Sahara Desert. He's the only one who can quench my thirst. He's always been my lifeblood. Being in such close proximity for the past twenty-four hours has brought everything within me to the surface.

I don't know how long we stand in our little faceoff, but it's me who finally can't take anymore. I don't remember dropping my bag, but I'm grateful I did. I launch myself at him. I throw my arms around his shoulders and spin us both so he's the one against the door. Even standing on the tips of my toes, though, I can't reach his lips. I need them. I need him. I've missed his taste, his touch, all of him. I've missed him.

Nico's eyes seemingly ignite in fiery passion seconds before his lips meet mine. He grips my butt as he kisses me until I see stars while he's lifting me. I wrap my legs around his waist. He spins us until it's me against the door once more.

"You're wearing way too much," he growls as he nips my lower lip and grinds into my center.

"Oh God, Nico." I push against his hard length as his lips crash to mine once more.

He reaches behind him and grabs my foot. He unties the lace with one hand and tugs off my boot. I gasp into his mouth as he tosses it back on the floor next to his own. He does the same with the other one, keeping me pinned between him and the door while he ravishes my mouth.

"You're not going out in this, Noelle. I'm not letting you." He doesn't give me the option to answer him before his tongue is wrestling with mine once more. It's a battle he knows he'll win. I'll submit to him every single day for the rest of our lives.

I moan in answer to him and press even closer to him, but it's still not enough. Trusting him to not drop me, I let go of his shoulders and unzip my coat. I wiggle my way out of it, being sure not to break our kiss. A kiss I've dreamt about countless times. It's haunted me, but at the same time, it's kept me going.

I toss my coat onto the bench next to me where I was sitting to put my boots on. I wrap my arms back around him and grind myself against his growing cock. I need him inside me more than I need to breathe.

Nico has always been good about reading me. He knows my every need and desire even before I do. So, I'm not at all surprised when I find myself floating through the air while his lips mold themselves to mine. Nico lets me down, but I'm ready to let go. I tighten my legs and arms around him, but I don't know how I stop myself from sliding down his body.

Nico pulls away slowly after I my feet finally touch the ground. We both are slightly out of breath, but there's no way either of us are finished with each other. He lets me go, and I whimper at the loss of his touch, but it's short lived. Nico strips his shirt off and sits down on the couch. He tosses the shirt over the arm of the couch at the same time he's grabbing me. I can't help but notice his gaze hasn't left mine until this very moment. The moment they start to roam up my body.

"Fuck, sweet girl." He settles me in front of him between his legs. "We need to get these clothes off."

I bite the inside of my cheek to keep from giggling. "But it's so cold outside."

His grin is wicked and full of promise. "I'll keep you warm."

Seconds later, Nico has my jeans and leggings pulled down and tugged off. He tosses them onto the arm of the couch with his shirt. My panties follow, and I can't stop the giggle from bubbling out of my mouth. It quickly turns to a gasp, though, when he flicks the button on his jeans and his cock springs free. I don't have any time to admire him, though. He grips my hips and has me straddling him faster than I can show his dick any appreciation.

"Too many clothes still," I whisper. The tip of his dick is nudging my pussy, waiting to be granted entrance.

"Agreed." He pulls my sweater off. The long sleeve shirt I had under it is gone next. I figure he'll leave the bra on, he loves it, but he removes that next. I'm completely naked. "Much better."

I moan the second his mouth latches onto one of my nipples. His tongue flicks back and forth as he sucks. My fingers tangle in his short hair. I tug just a little. His large hands move to my bottom, and he guides me down on top of him. He slides into my pussy, but it's not an easy feat.

32

I'm small and very tight. His dick is thick and somewhere between eight and nine inches. My pussy clamps around him. He'll have no choice but to work his way into me.

"Nico…," I whisper. I wrap my arms around his shoulders as tightly as my pussy is squeezing his length as he thrusts gently. I spread my legs as wide as I can make them. The wetter I get, the deeper he slides, inch by glorious inch, until he's buried balls deep inside me.

"Fuck, you feel better than I remember. How is that possible, beautiful girl?" He buries his face in my neck.

I love when he calls me that. He's the only one who's ever called me that. He's the only one I'd ever let call me it. I've never been one for sweet pet names, but when they fall from his lips, it's like honey that I'm on my knees waiting to lap up.

"I haven't been with anyone else. Just you. I haven't even touched myself. It felt wrong without you telling me I can come."

"Oh fuck," he groans.

I don't even need to tell him that I'm ready for him to move. Nico just knows. He begins thrusting slow and deliberately. We both hold onto each other like we need each other to stay afloat in rough seas. We breathe against each other's necks like it's the scent from one another's skin that keeps us alive. Each and every thrust he gives me seemingly heals another crack; another hole.

As he puts each piece of me back in place and repairs my soul, the thrusts get faster, deeper, and harder. The little bit of control I have is snapped in two. I hold onto him like he's my lifeline as I ride him for all I'm worth.

There's no talking. Only the sounds of him slamming into my pussy again and again. Our moans turn into growls of pleasure. Our lips meet each other's over and over, exploding into an inferno of passion and devotion. Our lovemaking is as intense as it used be, but it's so much more this time. This time, we're both pouring all of our souls and feelings into it. Everything we've locked up for so long.

I meet him thrust for thrust as I rock back and forth over his dick and slam down on him. My pussy pulses around him and clenches tighter and tighter, making him moan. His thumb touches my clit, making me jerk into him. With the perfect amount of pressure, he rubs. I buck into him wildly.

"Nico!" His name is the first word either of us has spoken since he dropped me onto his dick. "Ahhh!" I scream. My thighs tremble, followed closely by my entire body.

"Fuck, Noelle. Oh fuck, baby. Be my good girl and come for me." His voice is deep and dominant against my neck.

I've needed to hear that command for so long. I throw my head back and slam down on him hard, burying him as deeply as I can. "Nico! Oh God, yes! Yes! Nico!"

"Noelle!" Nico bellows.

I feel a river of come start flowing from his cock into me. Our hips jerk against each other as I experience an earth shattering orgasm more intense than any I've ever felt before. It's like the black hole in the universe exploded and sucked us both into it, swallowing us whole. Only the colors are brilliant, and it's not as scary as scientists believe. It's beautiful.

I don't know when he pulled out or how he got us to the floor in front of the fireplace. I couldn't explain when he started the fire that's currently burning and keeping us both as warm as we were when I was bouncing on him. All I know is wrapped in his arms with the blanket wrapped around us is all I've ever wanted. I could die happy right now and feel like my life is complete.

Nico is the greatest present of all time.

Chapter Seven

❄ Nico ❄

(Christmas Eve)

The next morning, after spending most of the night making the sweetest love to the woman who's always owned my heart and soul, I grunt and grumble as I drag a tree into the house as quietly as possible. The storm isn't slowing down. I spent a lot of time shoveling a path from the house to this tree. Luckily, it came down sometime last night, so I didn't need to cut it down. I dragged it to the garage to trim it.

I pause for a moment thinking I hear Noelle moving. After a few moments of silence, I continue tugging the tree inside. Thankfully, the garage is attached to the house, so once I got the tree in the garage, I was safe from the elements howling outside.

It seems like hours pass, but I finally have the tree up. I wouldn't bother with this, but I want to make this Christmas special for Noelle. She loves Christmas. She loves everything about it, but mostly, the time she gets to spend with people she cares about.

The thing is, she doesn't have family. Her parents passed away just after we started dating. After a lot of investigation, given they were only in their fifties, it was discovered that natural causes was the cause of death. She has no siblings or any other family that she knows about.

That didn't stop her from going all out for Christmas. The first one was a little bit hard on her, but she spent it with me and my family as well as a couple of my friends. She was happy with that during the duration of our relationship. I heard that the last couple of years, she spent Christmas alone. I spent it with my family, but still made it clear I didn't want to speak to Christian. He respected my wishes. The holidays were a little awkward, but we made it work.

At least I had them. Noelle had no one, and that was no one's fault but my own. I destroyed her, and then kept breaking her again and again with every single holiday she used to spend with me and my family. I went about my life. Noelle's was at a standstill. She volunteered to work just so she didn't have to be alone.

Not anymore.

From here on out, Noelle is never going to be alone again. I have a lot of time to make up for, but I'm willing to put in the work. She's worth it. She's worth everything and so much more. I'm going to prove it to her.

Once I get the tree set up, I go back to the garage for Christmas decorations. It may seem odd that I have any, I don't live here year round, but the last time I was here, the General Store was having a massive blowout sale. On a whim, I bought a lot of Christmas stuff. As soon as I got it back here, I sat asking myself why the hell I bought any of it. I played it off as I was just being nice to my friend and supporting his business.

I know now that it was fate leading me. No one really understands how fate works, but sometimes, she takes hold of a hand and leads. We have no choice but to follow, and that's just what I did. Now, I understand why I bought all of this stuff. It was to prepare for this moment.

Once I have everything in, I put my coat away. I strip my wet clothing and put it all in the washer. I start it and walk naked to my bathroom.

I peek into the bedroom and see Noelle still sound asleep. It's barely ten in the morning. I don't blame her for being out like a light. We were catching up on all of our lost time until almost five in the morning. The only reason I was up doing anything is because I couldn't fall asleep. I was thinking of all the ways I could make it all up to her and show her just how sorry I am. This was the number one way I could think of.

I quickly finish my shower and dry off. I wrap a towel around my waist and stride to my bedroom. My breath catches when I see Noelle putting her silky hair in a messy bun on top of her head.

"Goddamn, you're beautiful."

She lets out a quiet squeak as she turns to me. She clutches the blanket wrapped around her to her chest. "Nico, you scared me."

"Sorry, baby. That wasn't my intent." I give her a sexy grin and wink that has her giggling.

The sound goes straight to my dick. I ignore it and stride to my dresser. As much as I want to bury myself inside her again, I know she needs a break. Before she finally passed out from exhaustion, she whispered that her pussy bone hurt. I couldn't help but chuckle because of how cute she said it, but I know from experience that she's going to be walking on the slower and more careful side today.

"It's too cold for wearing such thin pajamas." She visibly shivers.

I glance at her. She's not wearing anything right now but my comforter, but I understand what she means. Her pajamas are a thin tank top with fleece bottoms. She expected to be in a warm hotel room where she can adjust the heat. I slide on a pair of gray sweatpants and remove the towel. She licks her lips and drops her eyes very obviously to my dick as I grab a sweatshirt.

I laugh. "I'd show you what you do to me, but I know you're hurting."

She blushes. "More just irritated than anything else, but you're right. I'm not sure I can take more right now." She looks down.

I grab her a pair of my sweats and a sweatshirt and walk to her. I sit down on the bed next to her and set them in her lap. "Put these on. Come out to the living room. I have a surprise for you." I kiss her softly as I get up, then kiss her forehead before I put on my sweatshirt and leave her to get dressed.

Not that I want to. I'd love to watch her. But I have one more thing to do before she gets out here. I hurry to the living room and put a couple of logs on the fire so she's warm when she comes out. I then rush to the kitchen when I hear the bathroom door close. I grab some bacon out of the fridge, grateful once more for the amazing community we're in. After I

37

start cooking it, I take out ingredients for waffles. I wasn't sure how long I'd be here, but there's enough food for at least three weeks.

"Thank God for that," I say to myself. I smile when I hear her come out of the bathroom just as I start mixing the batter.

"Mmm... I smell bacon."

I glance over my shoulder with a grin. Her nose is adorably sniffing the air. "Mmhmm." I turn and pour batter into the heated waffle maker.

This was a tradition I started with her the first Christmas we were together. She loves bacon with waffles. If she could, she'd eat it for every meal every day, but it became one of our Christmas traditions. Every Christmas Eve, I'd make it for her. And after I left, it was something I never gave up.

When I put it on my grocery list, I didn't think anything of it. Now, I feel like it was another fate thing. This entire thing was all something that was meant to happen. Maybe it wasn't our time then. I don't know. All I know is I'm never letting her go again. She's my forever. My endgame.

I smile down at her when she appears at my side. She sniffles as her eyes meet mine. "You remembered."

My grin widens, and I lean down to give her a sweet kiss. "Confession time. I never stopped doing this on Christmas Eve. I couldn't let it go."

"Me either," she whispers. "I thought about you all of the time. I missed you every day. But it was always worse around the holidays. Even though I chose to work and actually had a good time being around so many people, I still missed you like crazy. Last year, we ended up calling the police for something. I stayed in the background, but I was wishing so hard that it was you who showed up." She looks down and shakes her head. "That was so stupid of me."

"No, sweet girl. It wasn't stupid of you." I pull the waffle out of the maker and add more batter before turning and wrapping my arms around her.

I kiss the top of her head and feel her melt into me when her arms slip around my waist. With one hand, I flip the bacon, but I keep her close, swaying gently with her. She needs the comfort, and I just need her.

"I'm so scared I'm going to wake up. Like I'm just having a dream, and I'm going to wake up in my car buried in snow and you not being there."

"First of all, I wouldn't have left you, Noelle. I don't care if you were my mortal enemy. I never would've left you there. Second, this isn't a dream. I know because I've pinched myself several times and have the marks to prove it."

She giggles, and it's such a sweet sound. Seconds later, after she begins to pull away, she gasps. "Nico, no! You got a tree? How did you get a tree?" She squeals and runs towards it.

I laugh as I start plating things. "It came down last night. Luckily, the wind was blowing the opposite way of the power lines and the house. It was a pretty small tree, too. I think it's only around seven feet."

"It's perfect. And it smells amazing!"

I grin and turn with the plates. I bring them to the living room and set them on the table before going back to get some orange juice. Just as I'm opening the fridge, the inevitable happens. The power goes out.

"Fuck," I mumble.

"Oh no…"

I turn when I hear the fear in Noelle's voice. She's looking at me like she might cry. I smile reassuringly. "Don't worry, baby. We're all stocked up with gas for the generator. We'll be just fine."

She visibly relaxes. "You have a generator?"

I nod. "Most everyone out here does. It was the first thing I was told to invest in when I bought this place. Glad I did. It's come in handy a few times. Come grab the drinks. I'll get the generator going. I thought we could eat breakfast and then tackle decorating the tree."

Her smile is so wide. So pretty. Brighter and more beautiful than any Christmas lights in existence. "You have decorations?"

I nod. "I don't know why I bought them, but I'm going with Santa. He must have had a hand in making my wish come true."

She giggles as I wink and hurries to the fridge while I make my way to the garage. I can't help but smile at my analogy. Maybe fate has nothing to do with this.

Maybe it was Santa setting this all up all along.

Whatever it was, I know that it led me back to the other half of me. My home.

Chapter Eight

❄ Noelle ❄

(Christmas Day)

The entire day has been one perfect moment after another. It's like Nico and I are making up for lost time with the amount of sex we're having. The level of intimacy and love is what really fills the cracks of my heart, though. There's never been any other person for me in this world. Just him.

My Marine.

My protective, sexy, dominant, tough, perfect Marine.

One we crawled out of bed, Nico built a roaring fire in the fireplace for me. He got dressed in snow pants and a heavy coat so he could go outside and start shoveling us out. It was still snowing, but it had let up considerably. He wanted to get a bit of a headstart on shoveling.

I tried to go help, but he wouldn't let me. I don't have snow pants or anything like that. He didn't want me to freeze. That's the caring man I fell in love with. He never let me do things that would put me in danger or make me uncomfortable. I missed everything about him. I love him so much. I never stopped.

It didn't stop me from going out after a while, though. I stood near the garage and threw a snowball at him. I nailed him right in the back. Many might say that's a mistake on my part, but it had just the desired effect I wanted it to.

Nico shut off his four-wheeler with a plow on the front and got off slowly. He turned around just as deliberately and walked towards me, every step sure as the one before. It wasn't until he was almost near me that I took off running. I knew he'd catch me quickly, but that was my intention. We both landed in the snow, me on top of him, and then an epic snowball fight ensued.

By the time it was done, I was soaked from head to toe. He was still dry because of his snow clothes. He made me take a warm shower and get into warm clothes. I did just that as our Christmas dinner cooked. His friend who grabbed the food and made sure the cabin was set really did go all out. He didn't miss anything. I would think it was all planned, but I know better. Nico and I didn't start out on friendly terms this trip. We probably wouldn't be here had that storm not hit like it did.

I've never been more grateful for an act of mother nature as I am right now.

Once Nico was done outside, he showered and changed, then cuddled with me. And now, as Christmas dinner cooks in the background, I'm trying to figure out how I ended up so lucky.

Nico's lips find my neck, and he kisses softly. "I have something for you."

I look over my shoulder at him with a raised eyebrow. "What?"

"A Christmas present."

I smile and shake my head. "You. You're my Christmas present."

He grins against my hair. "I'm pretty great, but I do actually have something for you. Something I've carried with me for two years."

He moves his hand. I feel it against my back and hear metal clanging against metal. I look behind me again as he props himself up on his elbow. In his hand is something I truly believed he got rid of. Tears sting my eyes, and I sniffle. I shift enough so I can reach out and touch it.

"Oh my God," I whisper. I look up at him, my hand shaking as I softly caress the metal. "You kept it…"

He smiles a gentle smile and looks down and my fingers as I play with the chain around his neck. "I thought it was gone forever. I threw it out of anger across the room. Didn't know where it went. I found it when I was doing a deep clean a few days later. I don't know what possessed me to put it on the chain with my dog tags, but I did. It's been there ever since because despite the fact that I was so pissed, I never quit loving you. That made you feel closer to my heart."

I turn the rest of the way and wrap my arms around him. "Oh, Nico…" The tears I wanted to fight spill over. Nico's arms tighten around me, and he holds me tight as I let the tears fall.

Happy tears.

He's my calm. He's the warm to my cold. He found me wandering around in the fog and took me away from it all. I love him so much, it hurts my entire soul.

He kept it.

He kept my ring.

A few moments later, he's gently pushing me away just enough for him to unclasp the chain around his neck. I watch in fascination as he slides the ring off. My ring… The infinite, unending symbol of our love.

He takes my hand and slides it onto my finger, its rightful place. He kisses it, his lips grazing my skin. "Think you're ready to give us another chance? Or are you keeping me on probation?" He grins his signature smirk.

I can't help but laugh. "I love you. I want to be with you. Maybe just…" I try to look down, but he doesn't let me. He tangles his fingers in my hair and tugs so I have no choice but to look at him. "Um… trust… me next time…? I'd never -"

"I know. I know, princess. I fucked up. Beyond belief. I won't make excuses for it. It doesn't matter what I saw overseas, and how it affected me. What matters is that I took it all out on you when you were the only one holding me together. You didn't deserve that. I should've believed you and listened. Our break up isn't and never was your fault. I'm sorry I made you think it was. I'm sorry for my ignorance." His lips brush against mine, and I close my eyes briefly.

I open them slowly. "I never want this to happen again…"

"I'll spend the rest of my life making it up to you, baby girl. I'll spend every day proving to you I'm better than that. Because I am. I am better than that. I trust you with my whole being, baby. I'm sorry I lost sight of that."

I take a deep breath and slam my lips to his in a hard and punishing kiss that I know we both need. It leads just where I think it will, and before long, his gray sweats are pushed down over his thick and long length. My shirt and bra are up, exposing my breasts for Nico to do with as he pleases.

And the oven uses that very moment to beep, signaling that our ham is done.

"Saved by the bell," I rumble against his lips.

"Or cursed…" Nico grins as we both get up, and I giggle. We both arrange our clothes as we walk to the kitchen.

"It smells delicious," I say. "Just like old times."

Nico smiles down at me. "I don't know about that. My mom is the cook."

"Don't sell yourself short, my love. You've always been an amazing cook."

"Don't just flatter me just because you want my tongue between your legs again," Nico says as he takes the ham out of the oven and puts it on the counter to rest.

I laugh and help him put our candied yams, stuffing, and mashed potatoes to warm in the oven. Working like one unit, we move through the kitchen like a team until we've managed to get our dinner on a plate. We settle in front of the fire and put on Christmas movies while we eat.

The wind is howling outside, but inside, the fire is warm. The generator is keeping the TV and Christmas tree lights on.

It's perfect.

It's the perfect Christmas.

Chapter Nine

❄ Nico ❄

I grip Noelle's hips and slide her to the edge of the bed. I smirk darkly as my dick grazes her entrance and makes her gasp.

"Say that again, little blackbird," It's my nickname for her. Blackbird because she's exactly the opposite of one when it comes to looks, but she's fucking beautiful and sounds just as sweet.

Noelle giggles until she meets my eyes. It's then she notices our little game has changed. Her eyes widen, but I can see the fire behind them. "You're so good at giving me what I want… You… sure… you're… not the… submissive…?" She bites her lip and grips the sheets. She knows what's coming.

I grin wickedly. "Is that so, little one? You think I'm the submissive?"

Her eyes widen comically more, and I have to swallow down my laugh. "No!" she squeaks. "No! Not what I said!"

I tug her closer to me so her ass is barely on the edge of the bed. I grab her ankles and spread my feet a little so my cock is lined up better with where I need it to be. I lick her foot from her heel to her toes while the head of my length teases her. I nibble the tips of her toes before giving her other foot the same treatment. She has soft soles, as soft as her skin. She's always taken care of herself, and I'm pleased to see that one of my favorite parts of her is still a top priority for her.

I let my fingertips leave a light trail up her leg as she signs and moans softly. She loves when I worship her feet just as much as I love doing it. Something so beautiful and sensual about her feet. The way they arch so gracefully when she walks… It makes me even harder just imagining it. So hard that I almost let her go just so I can watch her walk away from me and towards me again.

But I don't.

Instead, I swat her pretty little ass just below her dripping wet pussy. I know what that does to her, so I'm prepared when she moans loudly and jumps. "Nico!" Her breath catches, and her eyes flutter closed.

I grip her thighs so she can't move and slap her ass again. She screams and jerks into me, allowing my dick to slide right into her. Just my tip, but it's enough to make her clench around me and try to pull me in deeper.

"What was that about me being the submissive one?" I slap her ass again.

"Ooohh… Nico… Deeper…" She reaches for me but can't quite make contact.

"Who said you get to make demands?" I give her another slap in the same place and sink in further when she jerks into me.

"Nico, please… please…"

"What were you saying to me about being submissive?" I poise my hand for another spank and grin.

"No! No! No! Okay! Okay! You're not submissive."

"Who's the sub?" I ask, my hand unmoving and my voice taking on the dominant edge I know makes her quiver for me. I feel her pussy clench around me tighter.

"Me!"

"Who's sub?"

"Yours! Only yours!"

"And who's the dom?"

"You! You are! My dom! You're my dom!"

"That's my good girl." Knowing she's about to explode her release on me, I press my thumb to her clit and rub as I slam my dick deep inside her. I groan at the feel of her pulsing erratically around me. "Fuck… Good girl. Take that dick, baby."

"Nico!" she shouts.

I keep her thighs tightly closed as I pound her pussy. It makes her feel tighter as she grips my cock. The wet sounds she makes every time I pull out and slam into her makes me feral because I know it's all for me.

She's all for me.

Mine.

"Noelle, fuck!" I roar when she grips me like a vice. Her body moves feverishly as she writhes and thrashes, making the sexiest noises I've ever heard in my life.

To get more leverage, I put a knee on the bed and bend her legs back a little bit, keeping them both closed, her feet over my shoulder as I lean down. My eyes nearly roll back in my head the second I slam back into her and slide deeper than before. I'm a big guy with a lot of length. She takes every damn inch. With every thrust, my balls smack her ass. Her moans get louder and louder until she's screaming my name.

"Nico!" She's so wet, she's dripping down my cock. I start to feel my control slip as I thrust into her, but I quickly regain it. Even if I feel out of control, she'll never know it.

But I'm not gonna last. Not with how good her pussy feels.

"Say it," I growl. She knows exactly what she needs to tell me in order for me to allow her to come during a punishment.

"I'm sorry! You're my dom. Always! I'm yours, Nico. All yours! Please, please let me come!" Her pussy is pulsing so erratically that she's pushing me right over the edge with her.

"Good girl. Such a good girl for me. Come. Right now."

"Ah! Nico!" she screams as she explodes for me. She soaks my dick as I continue to thrust into her.

"Noelle!" I shout as I fill her pussy with ropes of come shooting from dick into her. My hips have a mind of their own, and I keep pounding into her while we both lose ourselves.

When we both finish, I fall on the bed next to her, my semi-hard cock sliding out of her, and pull her on top of me. My come drips from her onto me. I know I've made an absolute mess out of both of us, but I don't care.

We both needed this. I needed to claim her as mine again. I've made very sweet and passionate love to her to prove how much I love her. We've fucked, but tonight was a claim. A claim that she's still mine. Always has been. Always will be.

"Mine," I rumble into her hair, tightening my grip on her.

"Yours."

All mine.

Epilogue

❄ *Noelle* ❄

(One Year Later)

"Man, this feels a lot better than the last couple of years," Christian says to Nico as they settle on the couch with their plates at their parent's house. I smile but say nothing. I focus my attention on *The Christmas Story*, a family tradition for Nico's family for as long as he could remember.

"It does feel nice," Nico says. I lean into him as his parents settle on the loveseat.

"It feels a lot less stressful," his dad says. His mom smiles brightly.

I lean into Nico and try not to giggle. Getting to this point wasn't the easiest feat. Last year, Nico and I spent Christmas snowed in at his cabin. We decorated the tree on Christmas Eve. Christmas Day was freezing cold, but we stayed quite warm and cozy. He had enough firewood and food to last a while. His friend definitely must've felt it necessary to stock him up with stuff like he did because he knew the storm would be bad. We had plenty of gas for the generator to run for as long as we ended up needing it to.

A couple of days after Christmas, we were finally able to start shoveling out. Thankfully, Nico had a snowblower to make the job a little bit easier, but there was so much snow that we had to take multiple breaks. It took us all day long to get cleared out, and the power didn't come back on during the whole time. Neither of us minded that, though. We spent the rest of our time helping out his neighbors. It was honestly the best Christmas I think I've ever had. The sense of community was just incredible.

I wanted to go back this year, but Nico said this year there was something special going on. He refuses to even give me a hint about what that is, though. No one has breathed a word about it, but everyone is looking at me funny.

The wedding we were supposed to attend was delayed, but only by a month. We both attended, and it was beautiful.

And that is where the Christian Saga begins… and ends. I hide my smile in Nico's arm as he and his brother teasingly bicker.

After we got back to Vegas, a couple of days after New Years, Nico got a taste of his own medicine. He texted Christian about needing to talk. Christian knew that we'd reconciled because I did tell him. He just wasn't willing to forgive and forget without showing Nico that he could be an asshole, too. He didn't block Nico's number, but he never responded.

When the wedding came around, Nico got the shock of his life. He stood next to Aaron at the altar. When Christian started walking down the aisle towards them, Nico's eyes about bugged out of his head. While he knew Aaron is gay, he had not idea Christian was. Definitely not a clue that the two were together. Christian came out to his family after he and Aaron started dating, but Nico wasn't there for that.

It was the best kept secret for the entire three years they were together. At first, they wanted to see how it would all work before they said anything to anyone. When they knew they were going to get married, they had a private engagement. They planned it all out. No one was the wiser. The ceremony itself was so quiet and lowkey that they never even sent invitations.

Aaron was the one who said he was getting married. Christian never said a word about it to anyone. Not even his parents. Just that he'd be at the wedding. They both got their closest friends and family members to go to the wedding because of how close knit we all are. We all thought we were going to support Aaron. When Christian appeared, there was a collective gasp followed by laughs and applause. When Christian got to the altar, the first thing he did was embrace Nico. They exchanged a few words that made them both cry. I never asked what they were because it was a beautiful and private moment.

"Sorry I'm late, everyone!" Aaron's voice booms as he comes in. "Things got hectic at work. It was like everyone in Vegas went crazy at the same time." Aaron is a paramedic.

Christian stands and kisses his husband on the cheek. "Have a seat. I'll grab you some food."

Gratefully, Aaron does just that as Christian hurries off. We all settle to finish the movie we're watching. After it's all done and we've all had our pie, we start opening presents.

I rub my tummy. I'm stuffed, but I have something to tell Nico. I planned out my own little surprise for him, but I'm questioning if I should do it now. I don't want whatever he's planning to be detracted from. Whatever it is deserves its moment to shine.

Nico rubs his hand up and down my back. I lean into him, and he kisses me on the head. "Full?"

"So full."

He chuckles and hugs me tight as Christian, who's playing Santa Claus and handing out the presents, sets a small box on the table in front of me. It's wrapped in gorgeous gold paper. I smile when he sets one on the table for Nico. Mine is wrapped in silver.

Their mom loves silver and gold. We always wrap our gifts in those colors because it matches her tree and Christmas decor. Most of her ornaments are silver and gold, but I love how she always adds personal touches. She has personalized ornaments on the tree as well as ornaments her kids made when they were younger.

"Open that one last," Nico whispers.

I nibble my lip. "I... think... maybe you should open yours last..." I focus on the box.

"How about we both open them at the same time?"

I nod, but my stomach is in knots. One by one, we each open all of our gifts until the only two that are left are the ones to each other. I take a breath and reach for mine. Nico smiles encouragingly and reaches for his.

"Ready?" I ask quietly. All eyes are on us. "Maybe you should wait to open yours when we're home," I whisper, suddenly feeling awful and thinking this is a terrible idea.

Nico leans over and kisses me softly. "No," he whispers. "I'm way too excited."

"But you said you have a surprise… I don't… want this to interfere…" I nibble my lip. He gives me the sweetest smile, and I'm suddenly put at ease. I nod with a soft smile of my own. "Okay."

We lean against each other as we take the paper off the boxes. I'm stunned when I see Kay Jewelers printed on the box. I look at Nico with wide eyes.

He smiles, his eyes locked on mine. "On the count of three. One…" He grins wider. I'm certain he can hear my heart race. I focus on the box. "Two…" He kisses my shoulder and gets ready to lift the lid on his. "Three."

I shakily remove the top of the box and gasp at the black box inside. I nearly drop it, but Nico takes my hand and steadies me as he gracefully falls to one knee. I gasp again as I look at him, but I'm confused because we're already engaged again. We just haven't gotten married yet. He takes the black box out and opens it. I hear the others making adorable noises. Through my tears, I can see their sparkling smiles, but my eyes are on the incredible man on his knee next to me.

"I've loved you since the second I saw you. You've always been the other half of me. Not being with you -"

"Through complete stupidity and fault all your own," Aaron says with a grin as he hugs his husband to his side.

Nico laughs. "Yes. All of that. Not being with you made me realize that I'm no one without you. You're my entire world. You're my light. I love you more than anything in this world and would be honored if you would keep kicking my stubborn ass all through our lives."

Everyone applauds, and I bury my face more into Nico's neck, still confused.

Nico hugs me closer as he sits back on the couch. He kisses my neck a few moments later and then takes out the white gold band with diamonds and blue sapphires. My gaze falls to the ring I hadn't seen until this moment. It's the wedding band that matches the engagement ring I'm wearing with the single, blue sapphire.

I finally realize what he's asking me, and my breath catches.

"I don't want to wait anymore. I want to get married. As quickly as possible."

"Yes!" I squeak.

I've never wanted a big wedding. I've been putting off planning it because it's been what everyone else wants and not me and Nico. We're content getting married at a courthouse, then having a giant reception. Nico just made that all possible with this single action.

As I hug him, I glance at the box my present is in, and my mouth drops. "You didn't open yours!"

He laughs and kisses me. "I didn't. I had all of that planned, and it was perfect." He kisses me again and again before he finally reaches for his gift.

The nerves settle right back into the pit of my stomach as he pulls the lid. He stares at it for a moment before looking at me then back at the pink stick that's settled on tissue paper in the box.

His mom's hand flies to her heart. "Oh...," she whispers.

Nico looks at me with tears shining in his eyes. "Baby... Is this...?"

I place a hand on my still flat stomach and nod. "Mmhmm..."

"You're...?"

I nod again. "Mmhmm."

Nico stands and pulls me up with him with the most adorable smile I've ever seen. "You're pregnant?"

I nod again. "We're having a baby," I whisper with a shy smile.

Nico lifts me off the ground and spins around the room kissing me. The family, our family, cheers and congratulates us. I get more hugs than I think I've ever gotten in my life. I love all of it.

But not as much as I love the fact that Nico and I are about to start our lives together. Something that never would have happened if we weren't snowed in last Christmas. I'll never be more grateful for whatever hand Christmas magic played in that.

This Christmas, I have everything I've ever wanted.

I'm complete.

Whole.
Home.

The End

Next In The Snowed In Trilogy

Next in the Snowed In Trilogy is *Snowed In With The Stalker!*

I'm being followed.

Every time I look over my shoulder, I feel like someone slips into the shadows so I can't see them.

But I can feel them. I feel their breath on my neck; their hands on my skin.

No one can help me. The police have tried, but it's hard to catch a ghost.

That's what he is. A ghost.

My only option is to flee, so that's what I do. I have a cabin that no one knows about. It's not under my name. It's not under any name that's associated with me.

But as I'm running, I can feel them chasing me… Hot on my trail.

Who are they? What do they want? And why do I not feel scared…? Why do I want them to catch me…?

Preorder *Snowed In With The Stalker* today!

Snowed In Trilogy

Available Now

Snowed In For Christmas

Other Books By Melony Ann

The Beautiful Dream Series

Available Now

Loving You
My Love, My Heart
Softening Lyric
Undercover Temptations
Captain Charming
Breaking Boundaries
Crashing Into You
Tactical Inferno
Ravishing Our Queen
Cherished By The Texan
Unveiling Our Passions

Box Sets Available

The Beautiful Dream Series: Box Set: Part 1
The Beautiful Dream Series: Box Set: Part 2

The Crane Family Series

Available Now

The Reluctant Mafia King
Sweet Lies
Billion Dollar Love Story
Be Mine
Protecting Her
Dangerously Forbidden Love
His Heart
Love In The Dark

Box Sets Available

The Crane Family Series

The Deimos Trilogy

Available Now

Connor's Legacy
Aryan's Alpha
Kade's Redemption

Box Sets Available

The Deimos Trilogy

The Forbidden Temptation Series

Available Now

The Detective's Forbidden Temptation
The Running Back's Forbidden Temptation
The Prez's Forbidden Temptation
The Coach's Forbidden Temptation
The Tight End's Forbidden Temptation

The Lucinio Family Series

Available Now

Rising From The Ashes
The Player's Rebel
Encrypting My Heart
Fighting My Fate
Phoenix Rising
Defending Her Honor

Multi Author Series
Piper Falls: Firehouse 49

Available Now

Ignite My Fire by Melony Ann
Regain My Fire by Kindra White
Playing With My Fire by D.L. Howe
Fight My Fire by Darley Collins
Against My Fire by Anneke Boshoff
Relight My Fire by Louise Murchie
Harness My Fire by Ayana Lisbet
Quench My Fire by Havana Wilder

Piper Falls: Station 28 Series

Available Now

Embracing My Duty by Melony Ann
Torn By My Duty by Kayla Baker
Against My Duty by Anneke Boshoff
Defying My Duty by D.L. Howe
Leave Of My Duty by Nikki A. Lamers
Fulfilling My Duty by Havana Wilder
Following My Duty by Louise Murchie
Replete In My Duty by Stacy Kristen
Accepting My Duty by Darley Collins

Let's Be Friends

Follow me on

Bookbub

Facebook

Goodreads

Instagram

Tik Tok

Visit my website
www.melonyannauthor.com

Subscribe to my newsletter and get a FREE never-seen-before NOVELLA
just for subscribers!
https://www.melonyannauthor.com/exclusive-content

Join my Facebook Reader Group!
Melony Ann's Sizzling Book Nook

Acknowledgements

Laura - I love you so much. I'm so happy that you came into my life when you did and stuck by me even when I didn't think it was possible to go on. We've been together through some super tough times and still manage to keep breathing. If not for you, there would be no me.

Jason - You dropped into my life and became such an important piece of it. You've been here for me at my worst. You've seen me at my best. You always put me together when I break. I hope I'm giving you all you selflessly give me.

To my loves.

To the Bookstagram Community.

To my family.

To all of those who believe in me and support me.

To all of those who don't.

Cover by: Carter Cover Designs

Edited by: Alyssa Skaggs

About Melony Ann

Melony Ann began writing short stories and poetry as a child. She continued honing her craft over the years until she took the plunge and began publishing her work, despite having severe anxiety.

Melony writes contemporary romance stories that are full of suspense and a lot of steam.

When she isn't writing, she is loving her family and working to make her life something she deserves.

Melony believes that if her writing can inspire just one person, then all of her hard work is worth it.

Her hope is that her writing allows each and every one of her readers to escape for a little while. To dive into a different world one book at a time.